My Fair Weather Friend

Connie Storey

Illustrated by Karen Lang

ISBNs:
978-1-5356-0419-2 (paperback)
978-1-5356-0420-8 (hardcover)

A special thanks to Mrs. Corn for her inspiration behind the story and my loving husband and kids for their support!

I have a friend
named Miss Priss.

She is not just any type of friend;
she helps me predict the weather!

Every morning, I let her outside and her reaction tells me what it's like outside.

If it's drizzling or raining, she will shake her whole body back and forth.

If it's sunny and warm, she will roll on her back on the patio.

If it's cold, she will run right back in the house!

If it's snowing, she flicks the snow off her paws to get the wet stuff off!

If it's really hot outside, she will run to the shade and stretch out to cool off.

If it's cloudy and a little chilly, she will curl up in a ball to stay warm.

If it's storming, she will refuse to go outside and run away from me!

I don't know what I would do without her help every morning.

Meet the Author:

Connie Storey is a first time author who has always dreamed of writing for children and young adults. She is married with two children, two cats, and two dogs from DeKalb, Illinois. She works as a fitness instructor. In her spare time she enjoys swimming, running, biking, dancing, reading and watching movies.

Meet the Illustrator:

Karen Lang lives in Sycamore IL with her husband Curt. They are a retired hygienist and dentist who now find time for the sweetest things—sharing life with their 3 kids and their spouses and 9 grandchildren. Their days are filled with ballgames, recitals, storytelling, cooking, art classes, gardening, and bringing life back to old forgotten buildings. Karen says of her paintings: "My Art flows out of my love for my God, creator of all things beautiful. It brings me joy, and I am so thrilled to share it with you."

Made in the USA
Columbia, SC
25 April 2017